When I Feel Jealous

WRITTEN BY Cornelia Maude Spelman

ILLUSTRATED BY Kathy Parkinson

Albert Whitman & Company
Morton Grove, Illinois

For that child who sometimes feels jealous.—C.M.S.
For Tansy, with lots of love and pats.—K.P.

Books by Cornelia Maude Spelman
After Charlotte's Mom Died ~ Mama and Daddy Bear's Divorce
Your Body Belongs to You

The Way I Feel Books:
When I Care about Others ~ When I Feel Jealous
When I Feel Angry ~ When I Feel Sad
When I Feel Good about Myself ~ When I Feel Scared

Library of Congress Cataloging-in-Publication Data

Spelman, Cornelia.
When I feel jealous / by Cornelia Maude Spelman ; illustrated by Kathy Parkinson.
p. cm. — (The way I feel)
Summary: A young bear describes situations that make her jealous, how it feels to be jealous, and how she can feel better.
ISBN 0-8075-8886-5 (hardcover)
[1. Jealousy—Fiction. 2. Bears—Fiction.] I. Parkinson, Kathy, ill. II. Title. III. Series.
PZ7.S74727Whk 2003 [E] — dc21 2003000239

The design is by Carol Gildar.

For more information about Albert Whitman & Company,
please visit our web site at www.albertwhitman.com.
Please visit Cornelia at her web site: www.corneliaspelman.com.

Note to Parents and Teachers

"Jealousy is a prickly, hot, horrible feeling." We all can probably relate to this description of one of our most unpleasant emotions. Yet jealousy is universal and unavoidable—even animals (as anyone who has a pet can attest) act jealous.

When we were children, we may have been told that it was "not nice" to feel jealous. Perhaps we learned to feel ashamed of such a "not-nice" feeling. But feelings are just feelings, neither good nor bad, and jealousy is one of them. Like the others, it can be acknowledged (not necessarily to the one of whom we are jealous, but to someone) and managed. In order for us to help our children with their jealousy, we first need to become accepting of our own.

Jealousy arises in situations that cause us to question our importance to others—are we okay as we are? Are we valued? Such doubts cause adults great anxiety; for children, who are completely dependent for their survival on affirmative answers to those questions, that anxiety can be intense.

So, to minimize jealousy, we can try to avoid comparing children; avoid setting up competitive situations where one child's "first" means another's "last." We can value individual differences and individual contributions, and reassure children of their essential worth.

And, when jealousy inevitably arises, we can affirm that while we all feel it, we can learn how to cope with it—without hurting others—by naming it, sharing it with someone we trust, and enduring it, with the knowledge that it will pass. We can remind children that each of them has his or her own way of being and doing, and that each child is unique and valuable.

Cornelia Maude Spelman

Sometimes I feel jealous.

I feel jealous when I think my mommy likes
someone else better than me

or when my friend plays with someone else
more than she plays with me.

I want my friend to like *me* best!

When someone has something I want, I feel jealous.
I want it, too!

I feel jealous when someone is good at
something I want to be good at.
What about me?

When someone else gets all the attention,
I feel jealous.

I want some attention, too.

Jealousy is a prickly, hot, horrible feeling.
I don't like feeling jealous, but—

everybody feels jealous
sometimes.
Children feel jealous.

Grownups feel jealous.

Even pets feel jealous.

When I feel jealous, there are ways to make myself feel better.
I can tell somebody about my jealousy. It helps when
somebody listens. It helps when they tell me that
sometimes they're jealous, too.

When I feel jealous, I can tell somebody what I need.
I can say, "Please be with me!"
I need to know that I am important to them.

If they can, they'll pay attention to me,
but I may have to wait.

Sometimes, I might just have to go do something else.

After a while, I start to feel better.

I can be glad when somebody else gets something nice.

I stop thinking about what others have or what others can do.
I think about what I have and what I can do.

The jealous feeling goes away, and I feel good again.

When I feel jealous, I know I won't always be jealous!